This book belongs to

....

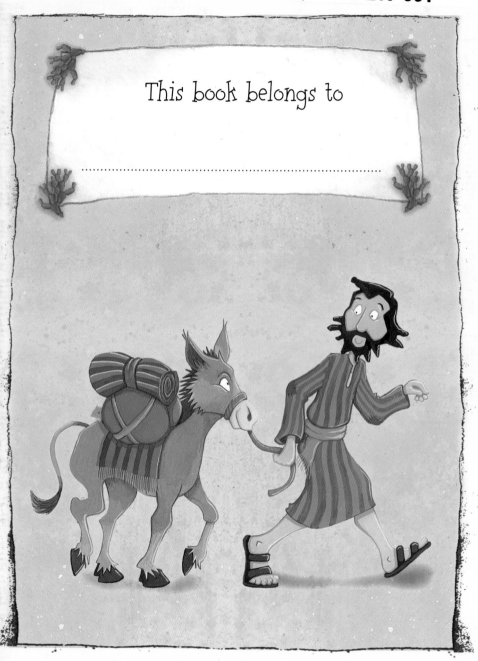

This is the story of Samaritan Sam,

Can you read it? Yes, you can!

There's something else. Can you guess what?

On every page there's a mouse to spot

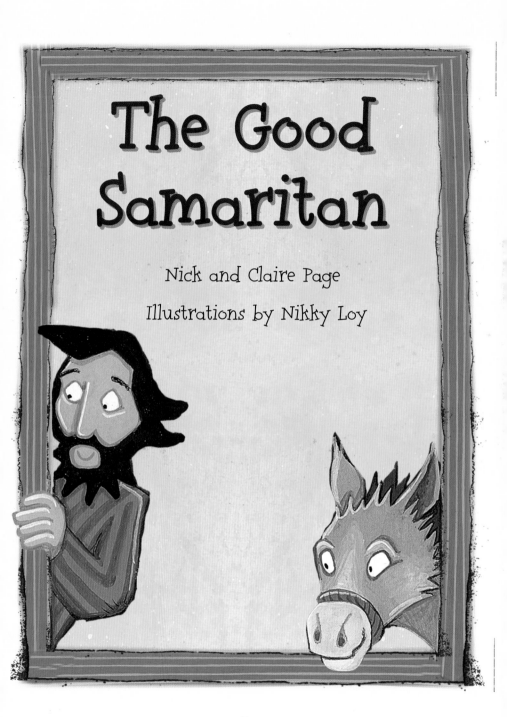

The Good Samaritan

Nick and Claire Page

Illustrations by Nikky Loy

make
believe
ideas

So here's the tale as I heard it.
There's this man, see?
Never done anyone any harm,
always minds his own business.
He's Izzy the Israelite. Is he? Right!
And he needs to get to Jericho, right?
And he lives in Jerusalem, see?

Well, it's a risky old road, that.
From Jerusalem to Jericho.
It's as rough as a rocky riverbed,
as winding as a wiggly worm,
as slippery as a slithery snake.

So anyway, he's walking along, is Izzy,
whistling to stop himself from being afraid.

Time goes by.
One o'clock: he's OK.
Two o'clock: on his way.
Three o'clock: it's a nice day –
blue skies above, sun shining down,
and only the rocks for shade.

Suddenly Izzy the Israelite notices
a flicker in the shadows.
Izzy's not alone. Is he? No.
There are thieves in the thickets,
robbers in the rocks,
bandits behind the boulders.

Robbers rush at him.

BIP! BAP! BOUF!

Thieves thump him.

OW! OUCH! OOF!

Bandits bash him and beat him up badly.

They take all his money, dump him in

a ditch and run away.

He's dizzy, is Izzy.
Is he? Very.
Perhaps someone will
walk by and help him.

Time goes by.
Four o'clock: no one near.
Five o'clock: sheds a tear.
Six o'clock: someone's here!

Here comes Parish the priest.

"He's holy! He'll help," says Izzy to himself.
Parish the priest sees Izzy lying by the side
of the road. And he crosses over to the other
side and keeps on walking!

I ask you! Is that properly priestly?
Is that godly and good? No.

Time goes by.
Seven o'clock: still no news.
Eight o'clock: badly bruised.
Nine o'clock: the sound of shoes.

Here comes Harris the temple helper.
"He's holy! He'll help," says Izzy to himself.
Harris the helper sees Izzy lying by the
side of the road. And he crosses over to
the other side and keeps on walking!
I ask you! Is that helpfully holy?
Is that godly and good? No.

Time goes by.
Ten o'clock: no light.
Eleven o'clock: what a fright!
Twelve o'clock: midnight.
Then along the road comes
Sam the Samaritan.
"He's horrible. He won't help,"
says Izzy to himself.

Now, as you know, Samaritans and Israelites,
they don't get along.
They fight like cats and dogs,
like lions and bears,
like... Israelites and Samaritans.
They're always arguing and forever fighting.

Would someone from Samaria
help someone from Israel?
What would you say?
Would someone from Israel
help someone from Samaria?
No way.

But when Sam the Samaritan sees
Izzy the Israelite lying by the side
of the road, he stops.
He steps over.
He stoops down to have a closer look.

Then Sam the Samaritan picks Izzy up and
washes out his wounds,
bandages his bruises,
cleans up his cuts.

Then he takes Izzy to a nearby inn
where he nurses him through the night
to the new day.
I ask you! Is that helpfully holy?
Is that godly and good? Yes!

And the next morning, Sam, he says to
the innkeeper, "Here is some money to look
after Izzy. If he needs anything more,
give him the goods,
add it to my bill,
I'll repay you when I return."
Then he goes on his way.

RECEPTION

And that's the tale as I heard it.
Now I ask you this.
Who showed lots of love?
Who scored the highest in holiness?
Who was godly and good?
Not Parish the priest;
Not Harris the temple helper;
But Sam, the very, very
good Samaritan.

Ready to tell

Oh no! Some of the pictures from this story have been mixed up! Can you retell the story and point to each picture in the correct order?

RECEPTION

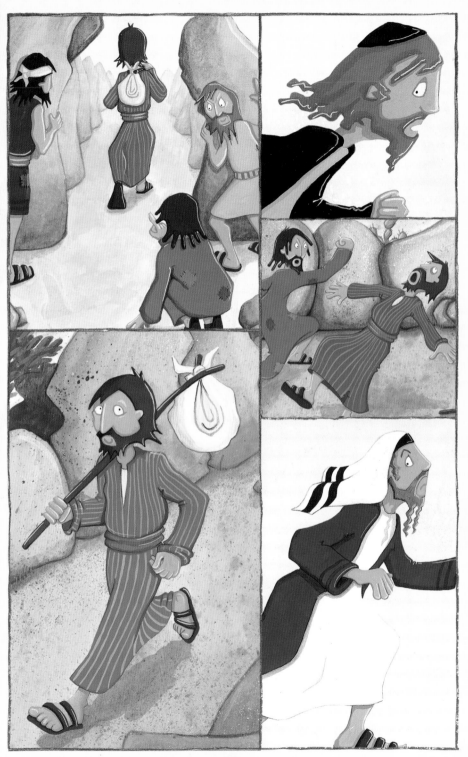

Picture dictionary

Encourage your child to read these harder words from the story and gradually develop their basic vocabulary.

bandage

boulders

donkey

money

road

robbers

rocks

thicket

walking

I up look we like and on at for

Key words

Here are some key words used in context. Help your child to use other words from the border in simple sentences.

Izzy was walking **to** Jericho.

"**We** will rob him," they said.

"Please help **me**," Izzy cried.

The priest walked **away**.

This man helped Izzy.

a he is said go you are this going they away play cat to

am can yes it see she or me was went in come get aay

the dog big my mom no dad all

Wicked wounds!

If you're play acting and want to pretend that you've been in a fight, like Izzy, here are some useful tips.

You will need

1 tbs petroleum jelly • a pinch of cocoa powder • red and blue food coloring • a bowl • facial tissues

What to do

1 Place petroleum jelly in a bowl.
2 Add a drop of food coloring (red and blue) and mix. Stir in the cocoa powder to make a dark blood color.
3 Separate a tissue. Using one layer, tear the tissue into a small rectangle and place on the wound site.
4 Cover the tissue with petroleum jelly and mold into the shape of a wound with a dip in the middle.
5 Fill the middle with the petroleum jelly mixture.

Other gruesome ideas

You can make fake, runny blood by mixing red and blue food coloring with a little clear honey and a drop or two of liquid soap.
Use yellow, brown, purple, and blue eyeshadow and blush to create convincing bruises.

Take care: Food coloring may stain clothing or fabric. Use soap and warm water to wash off the makeup.